$$t(x^2) \div \sqrt{9\,y(x)} = p4^2$$

a

b

e

h

c

$x + c/2$

c

$$4.729 - 1.3(x^2) \times \frac{6}{4}(y^6) = X\left(\frac{1}{3}\right)$$

864
792
46
420
c

$(x-j$

$fct\ \sqrt{6}$

O

$CH_2\ COOH$

oh)

$$fct\ \frac{y\left(\frac{6+9}{2}\right)\frac{4}{2} - \frac{x}{3}}{r\left(3x/2\right)+9}$$

a^3+

$j^2 = (\ \ )ra^2 - ab)$

B

$\frac{+}{6}$

A

m

$c^2 - \sinh(x)$

tr

American edition published in 2017 by Andersen Press USA,
an imprint of Andersen Press Ltd.
www.andersenpressusa.com

First published in Great Britain in 2017 by Andersen Press Ltd.,
20 Vauxhall Bridge Road, London SW1V 2SA.

Distributed in the United States and Canada by
Lerner Publishing Group, Inc.
241 First Avenue North
Minneapolis, MN 55401 USA

For reading levels and more information, look up
this title at www.lernerbooks.com.

Printed and bound in Malaysia

Library of Congress Cataloging-in-Publication Data Available.
ISBN: 978-1-5124-8126-6
eBook ISBN: 978-1-5124-8147-1

1 – TWP – 7/15/2017

FOR ARTHUR, SYLVIA AND FRIDA KATHRYN. THREE BEAUTIFUL BABIES - K.W   FOR ARCHIE AND ELLA - A.R

THE TICKLE TEST

Kathryn White

Adrian Reynolds

It's easy to **tickle** a tall giraffe,

she'll **giggle** and **gurgle** and chuckle and laugh.

a BEAR,
he'll jiggle and wriggle and bounce everywhere.

That gave me a scare!

An octopus
loves to be tickled for sure,

but which was the arm
that I tickled before?

To tickle a tiger,
hide under
his knees,

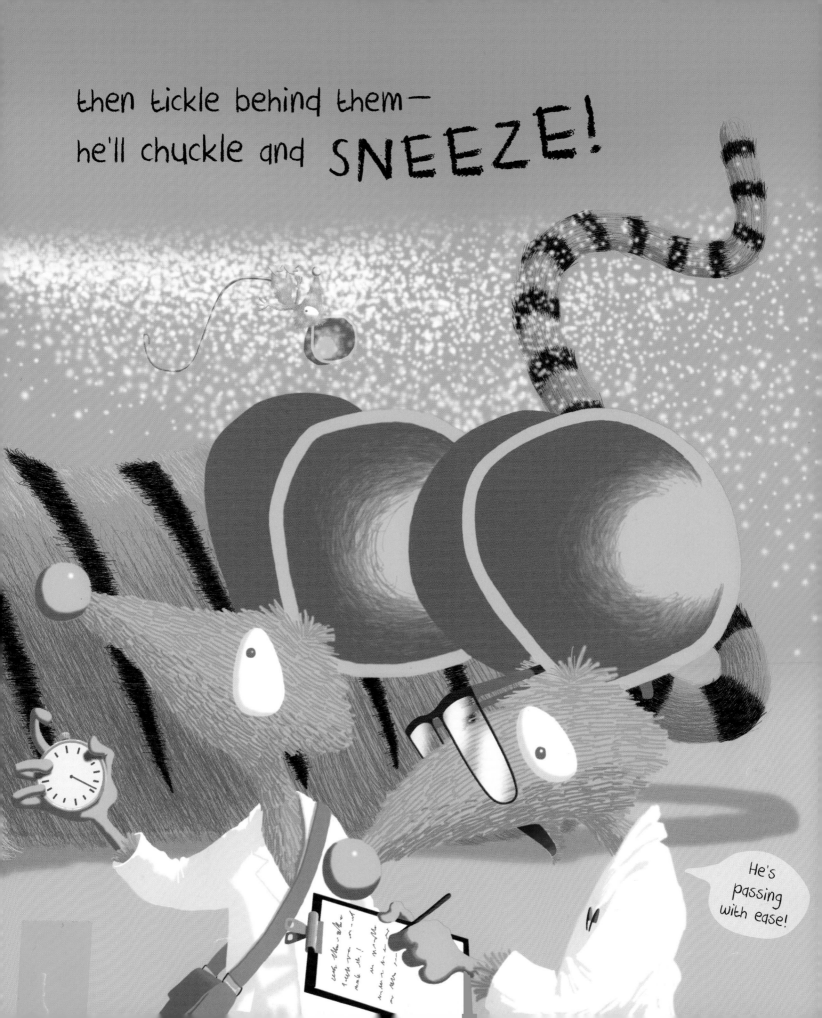

Creep up and tickle an elephant's toes.

Beware bottom trumpet— hold your nose!

Flamingos adore just a tickle or two.
But watch out for feathers or they'll tickle you.

And how to tickle a crocodile?
This dangerous test needs timing and style.

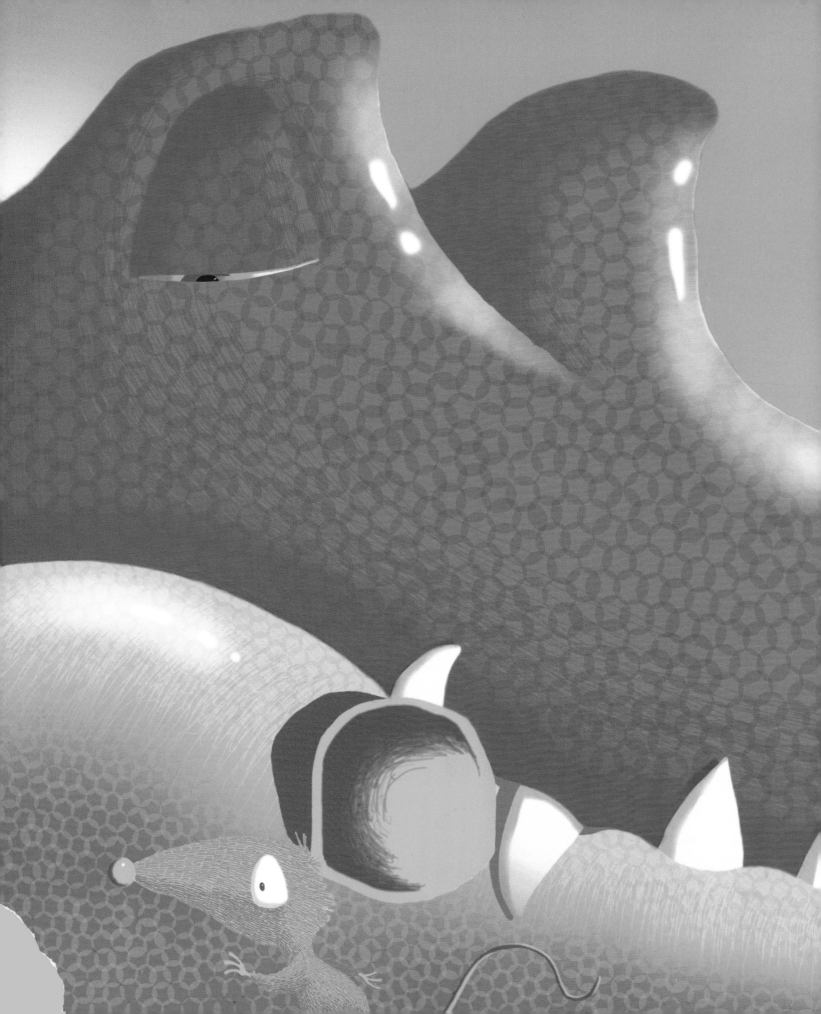

If crocodile spies you,
then you'd better dash—
those sharp teeth will
gobble you up in a flash!

He'll hoot with delight,
as he does with his mummy!
Tickling and laughing
are such fun to do.

So please tell us
just where we
should tickle...

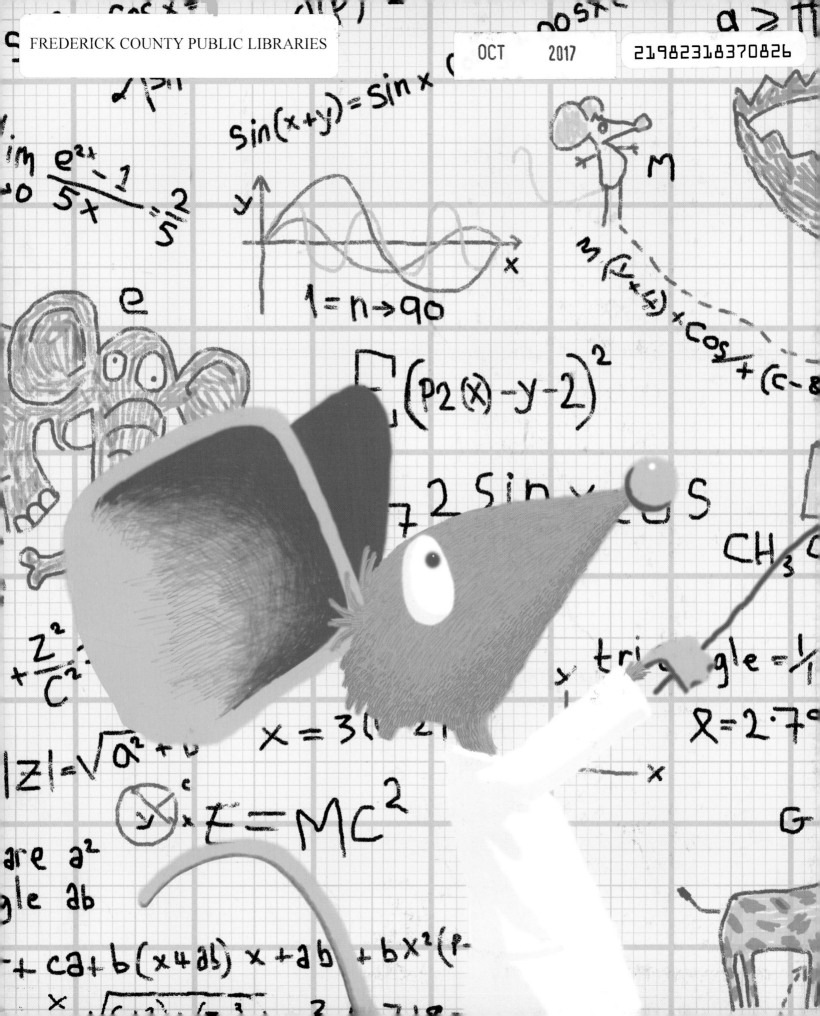